Voice

An Emotional Experience

AF382339

Copyright

 **Celince**

© 1937 Sabahattin Ali

Translated by: © 2024 Ince
Language of the original edition: Turkish

Publishing label: Celince
ISBN Softcover: 978-3-384-35210-1

Druck und Distribution im Auftrag des Übersetzers:
tredition GmbH, An der Strusbek 10, 22926 Ahrensburg, Germany

Das Werk, einschließlich seiner Teile, ist urheberrechtlich geschützt. Für die Inhalte ist der Übersetzer verantwortlich. Jede Verwertung ist ohne seine Zustimmung unzulässig.

Die Publikation und Verbreitung vom Übersetzer:
Yücel Ince
Saarlandstr.10
26919 Brake
Deutschland

Sabahattin Ali

VOICE

Voice

The truck that took us from *Beyşehir* to *Konya* broke down in a strait called *Barsakderesi*. The driver and his assistant opened the bonnet. They took out their seat mat, on which they were sitting, and spread out a number of tools, which they pulled out from underneath it.

Then began hours of repair work. Sometimes they both crawled under the machine, lay on their backs and examined the lower part of the engine with their hands. Sometimes one stepped on the accelerator and let the engine run while the other moved some porcelain-capped parts in the process. Under the afternoon sun, the tarp-covered truck had become unbearable. One by one, the passengers jumped off and scattered.

Some watched the driver curiously and as soon as he lifted his head a little from the engine to take a break, they asked excitedly:

"Ready?"

With a few less curious passengers, my friend and I, we went to the west side of the gorge to a shady spot, sat down on the stones and looked around while we waited.

A little further from where our truck was parked, on the side of the road, were two tents and all around a few spades and shovels and a wheelbarrow. Further away, a number of road workers could be seen busy crushing stones and transporting sand.

As the sun disappeared behind the hill, it cast an increasingly reddish light on the pine trees scattered on the opposite hill, leaving the valley in rapidly increasing twilight.

It was a cool spring day and the small river in the middle began to make soft noises. Some cars and trucks passed by. They stopped briefly next to our truck and asked the driver if he needed anything. A truck with free seats took two of our female passengers, who were getting more and more restless and kept mouthing at the driver, and took them to Konya. The other passengers sat in groups, telling stories.

An elderly man with a wooden leg, who had told us that he owned a grocery shop in a nearby village, got up, walked to the vehicle, shouldered his sack and went on his way after giving the driver a few swear words.

It was already deep in the night. The road workers returned to their tents and began to build fires. Our truck stood still like a huge dead animal carcass on the side of the road.

The driver and his assistant, covered in oil and dirt, with black sweat on their faces, sat quietly for a while and rested. Most of the passengers, who were used to such events, just nodded their heads and opened their baskets and bags to get something to eat. After a while, when it got really dark, the driver took a lantern from the road workers and got back to work. We passengers lay in the sudden silence, motionless in our seats.

The trees on the hill, behind which the sun was disappearing, were suddenly bathed in a bluish and pale light. I looked at my friend. He had his eyes firmly fixed on the opposite side.

The black pines scattered sparsely over the hillside drew trembling silhouettes against the rapidly brightening sky. After watching this for a while, he said:

"In a moment the moon will rise!"

At that very moment, there was a slight tremor in the air, filled with the scent of thyme and soft crackles from the gentle melody of a lute. My friend, who is involved in music and works at a music school, straightened up and began to listen intently.

The lute, which sounded from the side of the workers' camp, seemingly fell silent after a skilfully played solo, and a man's voice began to sing a folk song that had been unknown to us until then, but did not seem strange:

I turned to the withered leaf,
that fell from the branch,
Morning breeze,
break me,
scatter me,
carry my dust far away from here,
and rub myself tomorrow on the naked
Feet of her...

I, too, now straightened up. Although the lute had begun again with a lively interlude, the aftershock of that voice still echoed in my ear.

My friend looked at me as if to ask:

"What is it?"

"Excellent!", I murmured.

The voice started again, this time so loud that the whole valley seemed to vibrate:

With the lute in my hand, I went out,
to see the stranger,
returned to my beloved,
to lower my face in sorrow,
to ask this and that,
makes no sense,
look,
what state I am in without you.

I had never heard such a powerful, sweet male voice in my life. I was amazed how such meaningful and encompassing sounds could come out of a man's larynx. My friend stood up and pulled me up with him. We started walking towards the workers' tent.

Four or five people were sitting on the lawn in front of the tent. Spades and shovels lay scattered around them. A lantern hanging from the entrance to the tent, swaying in the wind, cast diffusely moving shadows that stretched into the valley and disappeared into the darkness. A young man who appeared to be no older than twenty was sitting on a wheelbarrow off to the side in front of the tent, playing the lute. His head was lowered onto his chest and his eyes were fixed on the ground, so that it was impossible to see his face completely.

His forehead, illuminated by the lantern light, was covered with drops of sweat. The long neck of his lute, under the fingers sliding rapidly up and down, trembled like a living thing. His right hand, strumming the strings, moved small but confidently.

Every time that hand came closer to the body of the lute, it felt as if there was a secret but very meaningful and important conversation going on between that wood and that skin. The tent and the place where we were grazed by a ray of light and stretched to the other end of the valley. We lifted our heads and saw the moon rising over the hill in front of us. The young man who played the lute also raised his head and eyed this bright, opposite listener with slightly narrowed eyes.

Then his hand playing the lute slowed down, his eyes closed, his throat tightened and his face reddened. As we watched him in amazement, his white teeth showed between his thin lips and the young man continued, as if addressing the moon, with his song:

The shine of the moon hits my lute,
no one talks about my words,
come,
my crescent eyebrow,
on my knee,
Envelop me,
the moon from one side,
you from the other.

The other passengers of the Vehicle had also gathered. They were all looking in amazement at this young man with the deep red cheeks. He had begun to move his mysterious talking hands over the lute, keeping his eyes on the ground or on his lute, which seemed to be bouncing in his lap. After a very short pause, this time without lifting his head, he read in a slower but equally sweet and deep voice:

For eight years I did not visit my home country,
I didn't look for a fellow sufferer for my suffering,
if one day you follow me again,
ask your heart for me,
not a servant.

And he put his lute beside him, after striking it twice hard, and raised his head. Some of those present shouted, "Bravo!" He began to let his eyes wander without directing them at anyone. He also tried to smile slightly. My friend approached him and asked:

"What's your name, boy?"

"Ali!"

"Where are you from?"

"I am from Sivas!"

"Where did you learn the lute?"

"I don't know... I've been playing since I was little."

"And the singing?"

"Same... Then I hung out with some master bards for a while."

My friend looked at me:

"An extraordinary voice, my friend, we could search for years and not find such a voice. I will not let go of this boy!" he said.

Then he asked his age again. He was twenty-two.

He pulled his notebook out of his pocket, made some

notes and wanted to know the boy's address. The boy was confused at first. He had no address to give.

He worked as a day labourer, here today, there tomorrow.

"Would it be enough if you said 'Ali from Sivas on his way to Beyşehir'?" he asked.

Finally, he gave the name of a hostel in Konya where he used to go.

My friend also noted that.

Meanwhile, the driver, who had been standing next to us for a long time and listening to the sounds with us, said:

"Gentlemen, the vehicle is ready!"

My friend, who was about to let the boy sing a few more songs, saw that the other passengers immediately jumped from their seats and grabbed their bags and suitcases and made their way towards the truck, sighed, then turned to Ali, who had already stood up:

"If I let you search and find me, come right away. I'll find you a paying job, you work alongside better bards, improve your lute, wouldn't that be great?"

Ali agreed without really understanding anything! He slapped him on the shoulder and said:

"Let's go, goodbye!"

All the workers said at the same time, "Drive safely!" and as we left, they gathered around Ali and started talking to him laughing. They were probably trying to explain my friend's words among themselves and get brilliant results for Ali out of it.

After he arrived in Ankara, my friend was very busy working for the young man. He was determined to train him in a music school. When we talked to him about this work he was so committed to:

"You don't understand, my brother," he would say when we talked about this matter.

"I can't get the boy's voice out of my head, I'm not a novice in this business, I can say I'm more or less a connoisseur of the human voice, but I've rarely heard a voice like that."

Although I felt the same way, I tried to look smarter and said:

"You are right. But didn't the night we heard him have any influence on the fact that his voice made such a strong impression on us? The moon! The soft murmur of a small river that was sometimes heard and sometimes disappeared.... The narrow, winding valley between two mountains and finally a voice that radiated out into nature from a worker's tent that we had not expected.... All this threw us into the frightened silence of that night and made us feel a strange romance, and did a voice, ordinary or a little better, make us think it was not extraordinary?"

But still, finding Ali from Sivas, bringing him to

Ankara and letting him hear again here to train and develop his voice was not a rejectable idea. Even if we had been wrong, we could not deny that we had stumbled upon a first-class talent. My friend was already swimming in dreams.

He thought that Ali from Sivas would one day give concerts in the cities of Europe as a famous and world-famous opera tenor:

"Seeing his body in tails and his red face peeking out from the white collar will be something wonderful!" he said.

Finally, he succeeded in getting his wish. Through many applications, he ensured that Ali was brought from Sivas to Ankara. The relevant authorities were looking for new talent anyway. Examinations were held regularly and pupils were selected to raise opera singers. It was in this context that Konya was written to. After a not too long search, our young tenor was found. The travel money was provided by the Konya municipality and he was sent to Ankara.

As soon as I entered the headmaster's office where the examination was to take place, I immediately recognised Ali from Sivas, who was waiting in a corner with his lute in his hand. His face was a little redder, his look clearly more anxious. Through the back of his flat shoes, you could see his holes in his socks and he changed feet frequently, as if the carpet beneath him was burning them. He had his lute leaning against the side of his right foot like a weapon and gripped his neck with two fingers. He did not look at the faces of the people talking and laughing in the room, but let his eyes wander on the floor and on the opposite wall.

After greeting the people in the room, I chatted with Ali. I asked him how the trip had gone. "Not bad!" he said.

The lute in his hand was new. I looked at him with a smile and he understood immediately:

"I found it at the hostel where I was staying. I spent eight lire on it. I suppose it wouldn't do to play my old, broken-down lute for the gentlemen!" he said.

His black and beautiful eyes, now bright and open, gave me the feeling that they were half-closed, just as I had seen them that evening. On closer inspection, I noticed that those big, dreamy eyes were constantly living in a dream. Suddenly I wanted to put myself in its place.

Who knows what he was thinking when he came here? Probably my friend's opera singer dreams and the ideas of tuxedo concerts in Europe were foreign to him. At most, he would have assumed that in Ankara a few "big shots" would listen to him, maybe they would give him five or ten pennies. He might even have thought that a more secure future awaited him, expecting, if he was liked, to be employed and favoured as a servant or porter and to play the lute now and then at "big" gatherings and get five or ten groschen for it. He had certainly heard that sometimes even governors protected such poets and let them play the lute at their meetings.

While the school's musicians from different countries were speaking in Turkish, German and French and filling the room, there was a knock on the director's door and two people entered. One of them was an education inspector.

He brought a boy with him who had just applied to the ministry and wanted to be tested. This boy, who said he had finished secondary school and that his teachers liked his voice, was a blond, rather plump, wavy-haired, confident-looking young man.

Those present said, "Of course!" They would check a tenor anyway; they could hear both together.

Finally, we left the room together. My friend opened the door to the examination room with satisfaction and confidence. It was a large hall with a parquet floor, and on one side was a newly constructed stage-like area. In a corner near the stage was a grand piano. The room filled up quickly. In groups, people began to speak in Turkish and French. Sometimes the discussions drowned each other out and the incomprehensible noise even gave me a headache.

A young German woman walked up to the piano and touched the keys. Ali cast a puzzled glance at this instrument he had never seen before, but then, probably to avoid appearing inexperienced, tried to adopt a nonchalant attitude.

Meanwhile, one of the young musicians said to Ali while placing a white lacquered iron chair on the stage:

"Sit down!"

Another musician stepped in:

"You don't sing sitting down! He should stand!"

"Have you ever seen a folk poet who sings standing up and plays the lute?"

During this discussion, Ali looked at the white, bare walls of the room, which looked like those of a hospital operating theatre, the large, curtainless windows, and cast anxious glances at these huddles of men who filled the room with their voices, like a patient looking at the doctors before being placed on the operating table.

I said to one of the young musicians next to me:

"It wouldn't be right to make him sit on a chair and sing, he's used to singing cross-legged, maybe he's uncomfortable!"

He looked at me for a moment as if to say, "That's right," but then he said:

"No, that would be inappropriate! We can't make

him sit cross-legged in front of the French! That would only make them laugh!"

Ali sat down on the white iron chair as if he were sitting on fire. His hand holding the lute trembled and sweat dripped from his forehead, his eyelashes and his cheeks covered with peach fuzz.

The speakers gradually fell silent. Everyone leaned against a corner or sat down on a chair they could find and focused their eyes on Ali, who was suddenly standing alone in the middle of the stage. The young man had his knees pressed tightly together and his teeth clenched. He took the lute in his lap. But he couldn't position it properly and looked around in confusion. When he saw the stares directed at him, he was completely confused. Sweat began to fall in drops on his yellow jacket. He took the cherrywood pick in his right hand and touched the strings a few times. These notes seemed to calm him for a moment. An expression of serenity appeared on his face. After playing a little more, he prepared to sing by moving his neck. He looked as if he wanted to cough but was embarrassed. Finally, he took his eyes off us and directed them to the corner of the blanket above us and began to sing a folk song. His voice was still beautiful, but it was mixed with some rough sounds.

These foreign sounds, which were not very noticeable when he raised his voice, showed themselves immediately when he went lower. Ali noticed that too. He tried to collect himself, but with this movement he only tensed the muscles of his neck even more and his face became even redder. He was trying hard. The round, folded pieces of flesh that extended down from the sides of his chin and stood immovable like two steel beams were clearly visible.

Ali was sweating as he tried to push his voice through this corset. Finally, he finished the song and stood up, the lute still in his hand.

One of the German musicians immediately said:

"Not bad, not bad... Let's hear the other one too..." and pointed with his head at the blond boy.

With a confident smile, the young man climbed the four-step staircase to the stage and immediately, without waiting for those present to fall silent, began to sing a folk song he had learned from a record. His voice, soft and sweet at first, gradually grew stronger and filled the whole room in waves. He sang really well. Despite some attempts to perform cheap tricks by imitating singers, it was obvious that he had excellent vocal material. No sooner had he finished the song than the German mentioned earlier shouted again, "Bravo!" - "We can promote this boy!"

At that moment, my eyes fell on Ali. As if he had nothing to do with those present, he let his eyes wander around the room, giving himself the appearance of a bored man.

The young woman at the piano beckoned him over. The candidates were to be subjected to an aural test. She played a simple melody with her right hand and prompted him in German:

"Repeat it exactly like that!"

One of the Turkish musicians explained:

"Sing in tune with the piano!"

Ali looked back and forth between me and my friend, who he was searching with his eyes. I thought, "Oh no!" The poor boy had been confronted with an instrument he had never seen, whose sound he had never heard, whose name he had never heard.

He did not even understand the meaning of the words that were said to him.

I tried to explain:

"My son, I want you to adjust your voice to what the lady is playing on the piano."

The woman at the piano repeated the melody and Ali, who was visibly trying, began with his neck raised:

"I sent a message to the land of my beloved..."

Some in the room laughed and Ali immediately fell silent.

"No, my dear," I said, "you shall not sing a song, but give these sounds of yours."

He let some sounds flow out of his throat and looked very strained.

One of the bored Germans beckoned the blond tenor over and said:

"Let him sing it."

The little melodies that the piano played one after the other flowed like a river from the young man's mouth. To end things quickly, they had Ali sing another song for formal reasons. This time Ali, who put in much more effort than the first time and realised that everything depended on this one song, performed his most beautiful song. It was not bad at all.

Indeed, those present nodded as if to say, "Excellent!" But as soon as the song ended and Ali pulled himself aside with his lute, they immediately forgot about him. The blond young man went back to singing a tango he had learned from records.

He undoubtedly had a beautiful voice. Finally, the exam was over and the discussion began about how best to promote this boy.

The question of the budget was raised. There was talk about whether or not he could be admitted as a student before June. No one noticed that Ali from Sivas was also still in the room. The friend who had brought him all this way stood next to the discussants and listened without saying anything. Neither he nor I dared to go up to Ali or even look at him.

When I slowly lifted my gaze, I was surprised. Ali did not show the slightest expression of misery that one would expect from a person in such a terrible situation. He continued to stare at the walls with blank eyes, as if the people in the room were completely irrelevant to him. There was no trace of regret or anger on his face. In fact, he looked as if he had just emerged from a long period of boredom and agony and was now in a calm and relaxed mood.

When his gaze fell on the blond tenor, he would linger there for a moment, perhaps watching him with a certain wonder and curiosity. I looked for signs of envy or even admiration in those glances and found none.

His lute lay like a weapon next to his right foot, and that foot lifted off the floor with a tiny movement and touched the parquet floors again. That's when I felt something inside me ache.

All the disappointment, all the breakdown, all the shattered hopes of the young man were revealed in those little foot movements.

This man, whose body was in full control, whose face could avoid even the slightest movement so as not to reveal his inner feelings, whose eyes shone with a gentle light of infinite depth and calm, revealed himself involuntarily through the tiny and nervous twitching of his right foot. I had never seen a human face or a cry that seemed so painful, so meaningful.

I collected myself and went over to him. I absolutely

had to talk to him, tell him something.

"Return to Konya, we will find you and notify you when we have work for you."

Ali heard all this as if it were something of extraordinary importance, raised his eyebrows slightly and seemed to want to learn it by heart. But when his eyes met mine, I was startled.

For some reason, those big black eyes struck me as revealing that their owner didn't believe a single one of those words.

To at least have the feeling of having done something, I suggested:

"Let's go to a restaurant and eat something!"

No one in the room noticed that we were leaving, they were so engrossed in their discussion.

We satisfied our hunger in a kebab stand, hardly exchanging a word with each other. It was impossible to fool him. Nor was it easy to say, "I'm sorry we called you and caused so much trouble!"

While I was thinking about it, we left the kebab stand. Ali swallowed a few times as if he wanted to say something, then lowered his head and said:

"I have embarrassed you, my lord, you need not be sorry."

Then he widened his eyes slightly, as if he were talking about something surprising, and added:

"In that room, I just couldn't find my voice!"

And then he left us.

The next morning, a friend of mine went to Haymana Inn to give him the money we had collected among ourselves and put him on a bus to Konya to bring him home safely. The innkeeper told him that Ali from Sivas had sold his lute for two liras and used the money as travel money. He had got on a truck at daybreak and set off for Konya.

Dog

It was a very hot summer day. Although the time was approaching afternoon and the sun was already sideways, there was not the slightest movement in the yellow grasses of the steppe: there was not yet a trace of the wind that usually began to blow at Lake Koçhisar at this time of the day, enveloping the vast plain in clouds of dust.

The Angora goats stretched out on their sides, spreading their curly hair over the barely distinguishable steppe plants, whether thorns or grasses. Drowsy, they kept their eyes half-closed and watched through their fluttering eyelashes a few white clouds the size of a palm hanging motionless on the eastern horizon.

Two large, spotted shepherd dogs lay some distance away, each on a hill overlooking the herd.

Although they appeared asleep, their ears perked up now and then as if by an electric shock, their small eyes sweeping the entire herd in a fleeting glance before closing again and their tired heads slowly sinking onto their outstretched legs.

The shepherd was sitting on a higher hill, leaning on his staff and dozing, while his eyes followed the half-metre-deep ruts of the road from Ankara to Konya, which ran about two hundred to three hundred metres away. There were about ten pairs of such ruts, and as soon as they got deeper and began to touch the underside of the cars, they were abandoned. Their task was then taken over by new companions who suddenly appeared beside them.

The young shepherd imagined how many such winding grooves could develop over time and saw in his mind's eye how these trenches, filled with flour-like earth that swirled up in gusts of wind and connected the horizon with a veil of dust clouds, could one day cover the entire steppe.

He muttered to himself:

"I guess the master will have to sell the goats!"

Even now, the animals roamed for hours, consuming the few meagre grasses they found before returning to the village.

In spring, the green, sparse grass grew only to the height of four fingers and was then immediately grazed by the goats, who were content with a few bushes that sprouted here and there and seemed to yellow and dry out before they became properly green.

But they didn't seem to complain. Despite this meagre pasture, they had long, silky hair. There was a broad contentment and relaxation in their eyes, and there was no other expression.

While the shepherd was thinking about the fact that the whole plain could be covered by dusty car roads and there would be no grass left for the goats, many other thoughts came to his mind: "If the Lord sells the sheep and dismisses me, will he pay me my full year's salary?" he asked himself. He was supposed to receive twelve lira a year, plus rations from the Lord, but he had not received any money for two years.

His master had said:

"What do you need the money for? Leave it with me, I'll give it to you all at once!"

If his clothes were run down, he would just give him an old pair of trousers and a shirt.

"It would be good if I could get two years' salary at once!" he said with a doubtful nod. He was eighteen, maybe not. He had a wheat face, open auburn hair and brown eyes. His somewhat protruding teeth and the eyebrows that fell over his eyes did not make him handsome, but he had a serious and dignified bearing that was pleasant.

"If we didn't have the old woman, I could go to town and earn five or ten pennies," he said.

But this option did not seem particularly appealing to him either. He remembered some people who had returned to the village more miserable, exhausted and hopeless after three or four years in the city.

They told us that they had found nothing but odd jobs and the hardest physical labour there, that they felt rich when they earned twenty-five or thirty groschen a day, and that they missed the warm straw beds of the village very much on the cold nights on the pavements.

"What should I do?" he asked himself.

Since his mother could no longer work in the fields, such thoughts were constantly turning in the young shepherd's head. But when he saw the condition of those who had thought and tried the same before him, he fell into hopelessness.

For example, a few years ago one of his relatives had decided to go to Izmir and enrol as a worker in a factory. The first reports suggested an acceptable situation, but then one day he returned to the village with only one leg.

He had got his foot caught in a machine; they had put forty or fifty banknotes in his hand and thrown him out. He went to Konya to beg. There, too, the municipality would not leave him alone. The poor man's lot was miserable.

Staying in the village and making something of himself seemed completely impossible. To buy a field that yielded little, he had to work ten years; to own a pair of oxen, fifteen years. And even then, it was doubtful whether life would become more pleasant. Those with a field and a pair of oxen were no better off than he. In a drought year, they too, like all the villagers, had to go to the mountains to fetch grass.

They also had to watch their oxen starve or be sold for a tenth of the price. Compared to them, he was even better off, because the landowner provided him with bread and provisions even in bad years. Maybe one day he would give him his money too? Who knows?

He let his gaze wander over the goats.

Then he called the dog lying on the right hill: "Karabaş!"

The dog immediately shook his head and straightened up. He looked in the direction from which the voice came, slowly stretched his legs and came to the shepherd with quick steps.

The other dog had also straightened up and turned his head towards the shepherd. Since he was not called, he was in no hurry, but carefully shook off the dust and grass that stuck to his fur.

Karabaş stopped a step in front of the shepherd. He

began to wag his furry tail slowly in the air and looked with waiting eyes at his counterpart.

The shepherd reached out and grabbed the animal by the foreleg, pulling it towards him. The dog, which came hopping closer on three legs, put its head in the boy's lap and stretched out.

His big body shook with joy and his tail bobbed back and forth, rolling the little stones on the ground.

Shepherd and dog looked at each other without making a sound. You could see that they understood each other down to the deepest corners of their souls and were bound together with a primal, deep-rooted love. A soothing breath that came from between the shepherd's protruding white teeth spread over the dog's face, and his pink tongue trembled as if sucking in that breath.

The other dog, who was standing on the hill to the left and immediately felt that the responsibility for the herd now lay solely with him, suddenly jumped up and rushed down the slope barking.

The shepherd and the Karabaş lying in his lap turned their heads in that direction.

From a distance, a cloud of dust rolled in from Ankara Street. As it got closer, one could see that it was a car. Now the dog that had jumped out in front of the shepherd had also run down the slope and reached the edge of the road - or rather, the roads.

Both barked with their heads stretched forward, waiting for the enemy approaching with breathtaking speed.

As the distance became smaller, they charged towards it. Meanwhile, the goats maintained an astonishing composure and let the now rather low sunlight shine on their long and heavily curled horns.

The car, a large closed vehicle whose light blue colour was recognisable even under the thick white dust, stopped before the dogs approached. They barked more softly. The shepherd called them from where he stood. They both withdrew slowly, glancing over their shoulders now and then.

The front door of the car opened and a young man with black hair and a thin moustache jumped out and beckoned the shepherd.

This young man was an engineer who had completed his education at college and later in America. He had returned home a year ago. Thanks to the intercession of influential relatives, he had quickly got a position in a bank that actually had nothing to do with his field, but he did not complain. Three or four books filled with mathematical formulae and signs stood untouched on a corner of his crystal desk, like eternal witnesses to the fact that he was a scientist.

And he, although he didn't quite understand what he was doing, completed some bureaucratic tasks flawlessly in a few hours and killed time by flicking through some English magazines, perhaps for the third time.

About six months after his engagement to the daughter of an important banker, he noticed that it was possible to organise his free time better. The car he had bought at that time and used for daily trips with his fiancée was unique in Ankara. When it appeared quietly around a street corner and disappeared with a beautiful reflation in its big body at another corner, or when it glided as if flying through the straight boulevard, passers-by inevitably had to take a look. Today he was on his way to Konya to visit an engineer friend who, like himself, had studied in America.

His fiancée and his mother-in-law, who thought it inappropriate to let him go alone, were also there. The young woman was pleased with this change and kept smiling, while her mother sulked because of the dust and the shocks.

After jumping out of the car and calling the shepherd, the engineer shook his legs and moved around to dispel the numbness. He was dressed in a grey sports suit made of Scottish fabric and a cap of the same colour.

Under his golf trousers he wore checked socks, perhaps twenty-five colours, on his feet he wore thick round-toed loafers with a fluffy leather cover.

Like anyone else who owns a private car and wants to live the luxury to the full, his shoes were stained with petrol and machine oil and the sole of the right one was punctured from stepping on the accelerator.

As he walked back and forth, he stopped next to the car and leaned his arms against the open window of the side door and said to his fiancée:

"What made you think of talking to an old shepherd?"

The young girl, shrugging her shoulders, arms and eyes, replied:

"I'm curious, I've never seen a villager before!"

The mother sitting next to her did not turn her head and said:

"What nonsense! Haven't you seen them in the markets and streets of Ankara?"

"Oh! Are they villagers? No... workers... But I want to see such shepherds. Then I will also stroke the little goats."

The engineer said:

"There are no small goats here, they are all huge!"

With every spoken word, every movement, indeed every glance, various parts of her body inevitably began to fidget. These coquettish movements, half intentional and half due to nervousness, were reminiscent of a ridiculous toy.

The young girl shrugged with indignation and said

in her thin voice:

"So what? What does it matter if I want to stop? I just want it! I like the way the goats lie".

In the meantime, the shepherd had come closer and the dogs had returned to the herd and taken them under their supervision.

The young engineer said to the shepherd who was waiting a little further on:

"Come closer! Where are you from?"

The shepherd pointed with his hand to a village on the north side of the plain:

"I'm from here!"

"Are these goats yours?"

"No, they belong to the landlord!"

"Do you come here every day to graze them?"

The shepherd let his gaze rest on his counterpart for a moment to understand why this question was asked and then shrugged his shoulders:

"We don't know. Wherever, we'll go!" he muttered.

The shepherd, forced to answer many more questions of this kind and unable to say, "What's it to you? Go on!" was deeply annoyed. Again and again he looked around to check on his flock and occasionally glanced at the car.

In the meantime, the occupants opened the door. The young girl jumped onto the floor in her white linen jacket dress and low-heeled stilettos. Her mother followed her slowly, holding on to both sides. The old woman's face was completely grim. "Why are we wasting time here? What kind of moronic children are they!" she thought.

The young girl came to her fiancé and clung to his shoulder with her hands clasped, then she put her lips forward and said:

"Look at me, shepherd!" she said. "Do you have a fiancé?"

She had read this word in some stories a few years ago and had memorised it.

The shepherd asked in surprise:

"What is it?"

The girl looked at the engineer.

He explained:

"My dear, a fiancée. Such a rosy, pretty thing. Just like that..."

And he pinched the cheek of his fiancée, who had rested her chin on his shoulder.

The shepherd grimaced as if he felt sick:

"Not a chance, my lord," he said. "We barely have enough to satisfy our hunger."

"Find a rich woman, maybe a landowner's daughter or something."

The shepherd did not answer. He stared dumbfounded at the mother-in-law. Earring-like clusters hung under the false curls of her dyed yellow hair, her eyes were rimmed with purple, her cheeks were covered with colour that resembled the colour of a cherry. This multiple dressed woman with her printed robe had suddenly piqued his interest. He stared and stared, unable to avert his gaze. Seeing that many of his questions remained unanswered and slowly being overwhelmed by the fascination of "contact with the people, the villagers", or rather being annoyed because of the self-confident attitude and seriousness of the shepherd, the engineer wanted to squeeze him, with self-control, but with an obvious reproach:

"Why don't you answer? See how we deal with you. You are our brother from the village. We are also one of you!"

The shepherd asked with interest:

"Who are you from?"

At first the engineer did not understand, then he said:

"No, my dear, not like that. We are also farmers like you, our origin is rural. I would like to say that we are all one."

The shepherd let his gaze rest for a moment on the three people in front of him, then he said with a strange reluctance:

"I can't tell, my lord!" and began to watch the mother-in-law again.

Now the engineer said with open anger:

"What are you looking at?"

The lady answered from behind:

"Where should he look, he's staring at me like he's going to eat me with his eyes. Is he a savage or what?"

The shepherd's eyes grew wide.

The old woman's mouth opened to reveal a lot of rubber, porcelain, gold and a few yellow long teeth.

The engineer couldn't help it, he had to laugh. The shepherd turned his head and looked behind him. It was obvious that he had had enough of this conversation. Then the engineer remembered that he had a social task to talk to the people and show them the right way and started to speak:

"Listen, my brother shepherd," he said.

"You are still very backward. You see! We leave our place, our home, to talk to you, to listen to your concerns; instead of benefiting, you just look around. What are your needs? What are your problems? I want to find out, you have to open your whole heart to me. I am your brother. Am I not?"

The shepherd had turned bright red. He understood nothing of all these words and only felt that he had made his counterpart uncomfortable in some way, which saddened him.

The engineer resumed the conversation:

"I am an engineer, I work for you; you are a farmer, you work for me. Could we afford not to get along?"

He wanted to say more, wanted to explain in detail. He was indeed concerned. At that moment he felt the need to communicate with his counterpart. But his inability to find the appropriate language, perhaps also his general awkwardness in Turkish, silenced him.

The shepherd made several short, dismissive gestures with his hand and stammered:

"I didn't say anything, Lord.... Have I done something bad, Lord?"

The engineer's fiancée had understood nothing of this suddenly changing conversation and was beginning to feel bored.

After exchanging a glance with her mother, she pulled on the young man's arm and said:

"Come on honey, let's go!"

The engineer opened his mouth to say a few more words. He found no words. He jumped into his car, started the engine and, after a moment's hesitation, the car sped away in a cloud of dust. The shepherd was completely taken aback in that brief moment, a feeling of grief he had not known until then. Vaguely realising that perhaps he had wronged his counterpart, that he had angered him, he thought:

"Did I seem like a savage?"

The engineer had suddenly flown into a violent rage. To be almost pleading for words in front of a simple shepherd seemed unbearably offensive to him.

Despite the brotherhood he had emphasised in his previous words, he saw the clear difference between him and the shepherd and muttered between his teeth:

"These fools will never become human beings!"

A scream from his fiancée woke him up and as he turned his head to the side, he noticed the dogs barking and jumping around on both sides of the car. His hand immediately went to his back pocket.

Then he paused. He thought. This movement, which he wanted to make unconsciously, seemed the most necessary thing to him now. If it were not for other thoughts, he would probably even have used his weapon against the shepherd at that moment.

He stuck his small Mauser pistol, inherited from his father, through the side-opening window of the car and fired into the open mouth of the pied dog; then he stepped on the gas and his car disappeared in a cloud of dust.

Karabaş, the dog with the long hair, had rolled to the side of the road and immediately lay motionless. The other dog was standing next to Karabaş; his legs, as if to prevent him from going further, were stretched out and waiting. The shepherd ran up to him. He knelt down and stroked the head of his beloved friend. The sadness he had just felt had now been replaced by a deeper, more fitting pain.

He saw clearly that he had nothing to do with the

people who had left, that on the contrary they had separated him from something he loved very much, and he stroked the dead dog with watery eyes.

The other dog also sniffed at his friend's face. The white, long-haired, innocent-looking Angora goats, who had now all stood up, stared in amazement at a cloud of dust on the horizon and slowly gathered around the dead dog, the red light of the sun shining on their backs.

Hot water

When two gendarmes arrived at the edge of the village at dusk, they got off their horses and handed over the reins to the coffee house apprentice who was coming towards them. They stretched their legs and began to walk.

The streets of the village were empty. The roar of a sick cow could be heard in the distance. The wind was moving with a slight murmur in the branches of the willow trees. The forest that covered the hills on the west side of the village moved like a cloud above it.

After the gendarmes had entered the coffee house and exchanged a few words with the coffee seller in a low voice, they went out and marched towards the village.

The houses were completely plunged into darkness.... At the other end of the village, where the forest began, they approached a small house. They did not want to make any noise, that was clear.

When they reached the fence around the house, they rose on tiptoe and peered into the lit window. Inside, a woman was kneeling and drinking soup. Her hair, parted in many braids, fell down her back. Every now and then she cast a furtive glance outside.

One of the gendarmes muttered:

"The pig's wife, pretends she knows nothing!"

The other replied:

"This is our fourth visit. We haven't been able to catch him yet. It looks like Ismail is not here this time either, but let's see!"

They opened the garden gate and entered. One of the gendarmes went around the house. The other knocked on the door. Inside, there was no sign of commotion. Only the rustling of the three-layered robe of the woman standing up could be heard. Then came a soft voice from the other side of the door:

"Who is it?"

"Open... We are looking for Ismail!"

A bolt was pushed back and the woman opened the door and said:

"Please search, Ismail is not at home. The last time you were here, I told you: Ismail hasn't been here since the spring. Is it four months or what?"

The gendarme shouted:

"Shut up, he's supposed to have been here for two days, we got a message!"

The woman replied in a soft voice:

"These are lies, dear sir, only lies! Ismail has not even been seen around since the incident. Who knows where he went? Maybe he died in the mountains!"

The gendarme searched the luggage, tipped the beds and then looked around. The house consisted only of this one room and a passageway. In the passageway was a jug of olive oil, a breadboard and some other things that were difficult to identify. In the somewhat spacious parlour, a mattress lay at one corner and on it was an open Koran.

The gendarme first tried to approach the matter gently and spoke to the woman: "Look, Emine," he said, "give up resisting. You have understood that nothing good can be expected from this boy any more. The state will not let you have him. He has an account to give.

Why do you pity the savage murderer? But you will say he did not kill for pleasure, he killed to save his life. Well, then, why did he flee to the mountains? Has the state no court?

They won't eat him up just because the boy he killed is the son of a big landowner! He would have served his just sentence and gone free. Like I said, leave him behind and tell us where he is, where he ran off to tonight. Look, you're still young. Don't waste your life... Emine, come on, Ismail was here earlier, wasn't he? Who told you we were coming?"

"I've already said it, why do you insist! I haven't seen Ismail for four months!"

"Emine, this will not end well. We are not here for pleasure either. If the lieutenant finds out we haven't caught him again, it's our turn. Who knows to which distant mountain post he'll send us."

The woman was silent and looked ahead. The gendarmes looked at each other. Then they whispered a few words.

One said:

"Was the tip genuine, I wonder?"

The other with a sly smile:

"Now we'll find out!" and waved his hand as if he were a master at it.

Then he turned to the woman and shouted:

"Open that!" and pointed with his hand to a small wooden door in a corner of the room.

After a second of hesitation, the woman went there and turned the wooden latch, and the door opened by itself. It was a small bathroom.

No one was inside. The other gendarme looked questioningly at his comrade:

"Where is he?" he murmured.

"Hush!"

He approached the bathroom, where a sooty pewter jug and a small wooden stool could be seen, and put his hand into the jug.

Then he pulled it back as if he had been burnt:

"What does this hot water mean?" he asked.

"Nothing!"

"Can't it mean anything?" and an understanding grin spread across his face.

The woman murmured, blushing:

"I wanted to wash myself with hot water....

"The time of day was not enough? Who are you trying to fool? If your husband is not here, why do you prepare hot water at night?"

Then he said to his comrade:

"This is the safest method! When I search a refugee's house, I look in the bathroom first!"

Suddenly he grabbed the woman by the arm and pulled her towards him, screaming:

"Denial no longer helps! So tell me, where is Ismail? Since the water is quite hot, he must have just escaped. He can't be far from here. If you don't tell me, it's your own fault!"

The woman, whose face had turned white as a sheet, tried to tear herself away and said tremulously:

"I don't know!"

The gendarme then abruptly let go of her arm and began to walk around the room. His comrade leaned against a wall and watched the woman's rapidly rising and falling breath.

The wandering gendarme suddenly stopped and called his colleague with a wave of his hand.

He spoke softly, but loud enough for the woman to hear:

"Ismail is certainly not far away. If he does not surrender to us, will he not come to prevent the rape of his wife?"

Then he added even more quietly:

"I will grab Emine now and throw her on the pillow. If she screams, Ismail can't stand it, he'll come wherever he is. Then you wait at the door to catch him alive or dead.... If she doesn't scream... Well, what the hell... Try her once!"

The woman had turned white as a sheet and was trembling. She was biting her lower lip so hard that it was threatening to bleed. She looked around. Apart from the four walls and the two gendarmes, there was nothing.

The gendarme who had inspected the hot water earlier grabbed the woman by the wrist with shining eyes and dragged her to the side of the room. The other gendarme took his gun and went out. But neither one nor the other could force a single word out of the woman.... She did not scream once, did not call out to anyone for help. A while later the gendarmes left the house, their guns slung over their shoulders, a sweet feeling of exhaustion on their faces and a slight fear in their hearts. Emine slowly slipped out behind them and dived into the forest. Ismail, who had been waiting in the bushes until dawn, approached when he saw that the light was still on in the house.

He entered through the half-open door with a strange sadness. The room was desolate. The lamp, which was almost out of oil, was struggling to burn with sizzles.

There was no one there. He stepped in front of the door and whistled. A fourteen-year-old boy appeared from the village. He came running and looked around. Ismail immediately sent him down towards the café.

He wondered what to do if the gendarmes had taken Emine away. But the boy came back within half an hour and reported that the gendarmes had mounted their horses in the middle of the night and ridden into town without taking anyone with them.

They then searched for Emine with some other villagers.

They asked in every house, called around in the forest:

"Girl Emine... Where are you?"

But neither that day nor afterwards was there any trace of Emine anywhere.

A night by moonlight

As he leaned against a high, grass-covered wall and turned his half-closed eyes upwards, he saw that dusk had set in around him. He took a deep breath as if he had almost reached his destination. In front of him was a bridge over which a railway line ran. He walks under it, clinging to the walls. His legs trembled and his chest rose and fell with a terrible growl.

"I could die here," he thought.

But as if they did not want this hope to live in him for more than a moment, some men appeared on the opposite side with bundles in their hands.

Talking quickly, they passed him by; a one-horse carriage coming right behind him bumped on the broken pavement and quickly dipped into the street in front of him. Here, too, it was not deserted. Here, too, there were people coming and going. The thick and dilapidated walls that rose to the right and left could not hide him from people's eyes. He had to find a more secluded place where no one would disturb him and he would not disturb anyone.

He began to move forward, tugging the shoes with holes in the soles like heavy chains on his bare feet and pressing his hand on his chest, which hurt as if it would tear when he coughed. He had been completely famished for three days and had not eaten for perhaps three months until he was full.

When he felt hungry, he would grab his stomach with one hand as if he were stroking it. Then his lips, cracked in places, would tighten and a terrible expression resembling a smile would cross his face. The excruciating pain in his abdomen had ceased since last night. In its place was a complete numbness and a little nausea.

After crossing under the railway bridge, he entered a dark alley. There were wooden houses on both sides and a few children and cats in the street. Behind some windows, women could be heard shouting, swearing and children crying. On the street, which was littered with dirt holes in places, he continued walking, stopping every few steps.

Just a little further... Then surely a remote place, a deserted place would come. As some girls in wooden sandals, water containers in their hands, passed by, they stopped and looked at him.

As he tried to walk faster, he was seized by a coughing fit. It felt like wire brushes were whirling around in his chest. Finally, he collapsed on the threshold of a house with a closed door.

When the coughing fit was over, he looked in front of him with watery eyes. Between his feet were aubergine and onion peelings and two knuckle bones. For a moment these disappeared from his sight and he slipped suddenly and quickly back into his memory, a feeling that makes a man on an endless road look back again and again.

More than five years had passed since he had left home. At an age when one is still called a child, he had moved to a foreign country, done all kinds of work and learned many things. In recent years, he worked as an assistant mechanic in a small factory where his illness had begun.

More precisely, the shortness of breath that had plagued him from time to time since childhood became a suffocating disease in the stuffy, small engine room of this factory.

For a while, he tried to hang on despite everything. He suspected that once he was caught in the maelstrom of circumstances, there was no saving him. But day by day he grew weaker, and the coughing fits that occasionally ran around in his chest like bundles of thorns and made him squirm until his eyes bled increased and intensified. His injured windpipes began to ache as he breathed in the humid, stuffy air of the engine room.

When he woke up one morning, he found that he could no longer move. When he wanted to get up again after a few days of starvation and go to the factory, he was not even let in.

The crash he had been dreading for months began.

For a week he got by on the five or ten groschen he had in his pocket. Then another few days of hunger... He had a wealthy uncle who had come from his hometown and settled in the city. He sought him out and knocked anxiously on the double-leaf door of the house.

They gave him a place to sleep in the corner of a shed for a few days and put out a few morsels of food for him. These five boys, the oldest of whom was twelve years old, harassed him with a cruelty he could not understand, pouring water over his head while he slept and sometimes even stabbing his face and body with long sticks when he was shaken by a coughing fit.

His uncle, who earned quite well as a wholesaler and came home late and left early, had never once asked how he was.

He muttered unintelligible things as he passed him, and after keeping his eyes on the sick man for a moment, he just kept walking.

One morning, still very early, he stepped out into the street. He paused for a moment in front of his nephew, then he said:

"You have been sleeping here for three weeks.... This can't go on, go and register at a state hospital..." and continued walking.

That same day, they threw him out. By evening, he travelled through several hospitals, leaving the door of each one even more tired and hopeless. For a while he was a burden to his fellow sufferers.

These men, each of them just as poor as he, tried to help him as best they could. But even that did not last more than a few weeks. Another wandering began. This never-ending journey, whose destination was uncertain, was perhaps even worse than the illness itself.

It happened that he ran down the same street fifteen times in one day, like an animal driven into a dead end. Sometimes he begged, sometimes he ran to escape the police and crashed to the ground in a secluded corner, shaken by a coughing fit. Sometimes, too, he collected pieces of bread and fruit bowls from the rubbish bins on the streets and in the alleys.

Even at that, his illness was an obstacle that tied his hands. Children aged eight to ten, clustered around the piles of rubbish, pushed him aside and even took away what he had found.

As he rummaged through the piles, which gave off sour and sticky smells, he hastily and anxiously hid a melon rind he got his hands on, or a bunch of grapes with a few rotten berries on them, or a can of sardines, still showing remnants of oil, under his torn shirt.

He retreated to a corner and tried not to lose the food that the hungry children were swarming around him like flies, eating and scratching with trembling hands.

But for three days he could no longer do that. His stomach immediately expelled the various things fed to him with who knows what reluctance and wanted nothing, not even water.

At that moment, everything seemed to become clear to him. This state was a sign that the end was near. There was nothing left to do but die. He took it very calmly and wanted to leave this world as carefree as possible.

A strange feeling told him that although his stomach was rebelling, he would not die of hunger, but of his main illness, the chest. For this reason he almost forgot about his stomach. The fine pains that had spread through his ribs during the first few days had now completely disappeared. Now all he had was his chest, his cough and his weakness. With every step he felt his life fading a little more, and he searched with a fixed gaze as if to see his breath coming out of his mouth in single bursts, his soul leaping out in pieces and dissolving into the air.

The weaker he became, the more urgent was his need to find a secluded place to die. He had only one fear: if he collapsed in a busy place, say on a street corner, people would stand around him, push him, take him away, not let him die in peace. He was afraid of being mistreated while dying. The thought that he could somehow be helped and saved was so distant to him, and the possibility that there could be anyone in the world who would care for him was so alien to him that neither hope nor anger could ease his heavy nervous tension during this endless trek.

Having seen nothing but loneliness in his life, he was not even aware of his terrible loneliness. He cast flat, indifferent and perhaps somewhat shy glances at the people who surrounded him as if they were some foreign substance, a wall, a tree or a dog. For him, there was never anything extraordinary about death. The thing he had seen most often around him from childhood was death. However, there was one form of death that gave him goosebumps whenever he thought about it. He had often seen ravens pouncing on the dead cows, horses and other animals in his village during the day and jackals at night, and how the next day there was nothing left of the carcasses but a few pieces of red bone and a few tufts of fur.

Without realising it, this fear now took control of him: he believed that these people, whom he did not know who or what they were and who were as strange to him as a jackal or a crow, could tear him apart and make him unrecognisable in the same way. By the time he stood up in front of the door he was sitting on, it was already deep night and darkness had enveloped the lower parts of the houses. A little further up, towards the rooftops, the light gradually spread.

He walked a few steps. A noise sounded from one of the houses, he heard drunken shouting and dogs barking from some of the streets. He walked with his head down. Again a high wall rose in front of him. When he had walked about fifteen to twenty paces along the wall, suddenly the path in front of him opened up. He paused as if someone had punched him in the forehead. When he looked up, he saw the sea in front of him, a few steps ahead, stretching to the horizon and gently rippling in the moonlight.

It was a wonderful night. The moon, which looked twice as big as usual, seemed to have jumped from its place and to be approaching the earth and the sea. On the ruins of the walls and on the heaps of rubbish, the cheeky plants swayed gently like the flowers of a fairytale garden.

The moss-covered pebbles, wetted by the waves that occasionally licked the shore, looked like gems playing different colour games. Everything was half drunk, half faint. Despite this stillness and faintness, life bubbled out of everything.

He stared at the sea for a while, at the moon for a while, and then he suddenly realised that he didn't want to die. It was quiet and deserted here. He could lie on his back in a corner, look at the pale stars in the sky and wait for the next moment. Still, he felt his aching chest calling for a deep, vital breath.

Tears welled up in his eyes. This state, which he had never experienced in his life, astonished him. Before he could think about it further, he was overcome by a cough that covered his chest and put him into a strange and unfamiliar sadness for a few minutes. His conviction that he was going to die was not shaken, but it felt like something incomplete.

There was something missing around him, he tried to think: a series of figures passed through his mind like a mist, some of Dorf, others recognisable as his mother, but he could make nothing out completely. Slowly he sat down on a stone. He didn't know how much time had passed when a figure moved a little further in front of him. Had it always been there or had it crept up slowly? While he was thinking about it, a slender female figure approached and stopped a step in front of him, her gaze fixed on his face.

When he raised his head, he first met the eyes of the woman in front of him. These small dots, whose colours were not clear but which shone with a strange light, moved slowly over his body. As the moon was behind the woman, her face remained in darkness. Her shadow fell beside his knee. Her large hands dangled heavily at the ends of her thin arms. On her bare feet she wore untied shoes with worn heels, on her back a short robe of indeterminate colour, darkened only on her chest by dirt and stains.

The woman took another step, sat down next to the man and turned her face towards him with a meaningful raising of her eyebrows. The man admired this face, which was now fully illuminated by the moonlight.

On this dark and oily face, smallpox perhaps did its worst damage. Deep pits merged in places and covered large areas. Her lips were drawn in two thin white lines and a sly, false smile, adding many wrinkles to the furrows in her face, reached below her eyes.

The sick man, who was struggling with short, exhausted breaths and holding on to his sides with his hands to keep from collapsing, trembled before this woman's smile. Deep inside, there seemed to be a sadness that stood in stark contrast to the terrible smile on her face. Only one thing was a little strange: the deep black eyes of this woman, whose age was impossible to estimate, shone with the freshness of youth and clung to him. Deep within them seemed to be hidden a sorrow that formed a stark contrast to the terrible smile on her face.

The woman moved a little closer and said:

"Speak up!"

She spoke it in a brittle voice and a distinctly peasant dialect.

The young man, struggling to collect himself, asked

after a short pause:

"Where are you from?"

"What were you going to do now?"

"Nothing!"

"Come on, let's go this way."

"Why?"

The woman answered with astonishing matter-of-factness:

"This is a very public place. Someone might see us!"

The man, whose brief flash of interest immediately faded, grunted with a curt shrug:

"Go on, go about your business!"

The woman laughed as if she had not heard the insult. She put one leg over the other and asked with an insolent attitude:

" Are you penniless?"

She made the sign for money with the thumb and forefinger of her right hand.

A smile flitted across the man's face. She put her hand on the sick man's shoulder and asked:

"Don't you have fifteen pennies?"

Then she added, as if to excuse the insignificance of this sum:

"We are humble..."

The man replied in a hoarse voice:

"Go away!" and made a violent hand gesture.

But this immediately plunged him into an even

worse coughing fit than before. He jumped up, doubled over, and his eyes searched the things around him as if he needed help. He seemed to have forgotten that the woman was still there. After perhaps five minutes of this seizure, he collapsed at the foot of the stone he had just been sitting on. His eyes had become dull, his face expressionless and drooping, and bloody foam was forming at the corners of his lips.

The woman who had waited in the meantime, undecided and standing, slowly bent forward:

"Oh dear, you are sick!"

The young man's expressionless eyes lingered on her for a moment, then his head slowly sank forward.

The woman knelt down and murmured:

"What did you? Why didn't you predict this! Get up, I'll take you over it, then you can lie down and rest!"

Then she added in a quieter voice, shaking her head:

"You must be hungry too!"

The sick man said nothing, straightening his head as if he were doing hard work. When their eyes met, a peaceful expression came over his face. The sadness he had seen in her eyes a moment ago had now settled into her dark, pockmarked face and onto her thin, colourless lips. He tried to move.

The woman held him by the arm:

"It's not far, right here!"

They walked about ten steps. The four walls of a

burnt house appeared in front of them. They climbed the two-metre-high stairs of the door, which was now just an empty hole, and went inside.

In one corner of these wall remains, from which one could see the sea through the large stone windows and which had no roof, there was a sack stretched about a metre above the ground. Underneath it was a small jug, there was a pile of rags that looked like a blanket and a goatskin blanket, torn in places, spread out on some straw.

A worn basket hung in a slat stuck between the stones of the wall. The woman laid the sick man backwards on the goatskin blanket, took the basket from the wall, took out some pieces of dry bread and said:

"Eat!"

The man raised his eyebrows.

The woman asked:

"How many days has it been since you ate anything?"

The man pointed his fingers at three.

"Then wait, I will cook you something warm."

The woman went to the opposite corner of the wall and lit a fire with some shavings. She boiled some water in a crooked and lidless tea kettle. After rummaging in her basket for a long time and finding three pieces of sugar, she threw them into the water and stirred them. Sip by sip, she gave the young man the sweet, hot tea.

The hot liquid that ran slowly down his throat seemed to burn the wounds between his ribs, and the continuous stabbing pain lessened with each sip. After drinking the tea, he slowly slid back and lay down. The grass beneath him rustled as he moved. The woman pushed the rags that were lying in the corner under his head. After lying in this position for a while with his eyes closed, the young man seemed to lose consciousness, but suddenly jumped with a burning sensation in his chest and coughed violently.

The woman tried to hold his twitching arms, looked around with confused eyes and kept muttering:

"My goodness!... What are we going to do?"

Until dawn, these fits were repeated several times. Each time, the woman caught his swaying head, wiped the beads of sweat from his forehead, gave him a few sips of the still warm, sweet tea and gently laid his head on the rags when the fit was over. The moon drew its veil of false beauty over everything and approached the western hill, while the peaks of the opposite mountains were bathed in a soft pink light.

The young sick had been lying on his back for a long time watching the increasingly pale and still flickering stars in the sky, waiting with fear for the next suffocating seizure. Finally, he closed his eyes and seemed overwhelmed by a tremendous exhaustion.

But after a while he came to with a strange feeling. At first, with his eyes closed, he tried to understand what was going on: drops fell on his face at short intervals. He opened his eyes slightly. A sweet chill spread through his whole body. The woman, whose face was barely discernible in the semi-darkness, bent over him, crying silently, only occasionally twitching with a sob that she tried to stifle in her chest. The young man heard a human heart beating violently above his head. He opened his eyes fully and looked up. The woman's brown, greasy, pockmarked face seemed to him beautiful enough to kiss.

On this face he saw traces of an affection he had never seen in a human being, an affection that reminded him of a sister, a mother, a lover.

This woman, who could shed such miserable, bitter tears by bending over a person she did not know what he was, who he was, seemed to her like a wonderful creature. When their eyes met, she seemed to smile, but behind it was her usual young and sad expression. The man felt himself falling into a weakness he did not understand.

He took her bony, large and firm fingers in his hands and pulled her to his chest. He closed his eyes and slept a peaceful and sweet sleep for the first time in years under the warm tears still falling on his face.

The beauty queen of Constance

I had just arrived in Berlin, a city I hadn't seen for four years. I had spent most of my time in villages with mud houses, in towns on the Mediterranean coast where the hot sun met the clear blue sea, and sometimes I rode from village to village on an old horse along heath paths. After those four years, Berlin seemed like a place I had never seen before.

On the stairs of the station, where I arrived at dusk, my feet and my eyes felt strange in the glare of the windows of a large casino opposite me. No sooner had I deposited my things in a hotel than I rushed out into the street without changing and began to walk slowly.

But the houses around me seemed to come to life and want to pounce on me; trams, buses, people in a hurry all started rushing towards me at once. I looked for a place to escape.

The smell of the crowd and the noise of people coming out of the casinos I was about to enter threw me back. In the venues I entered, I seemed to see that liveliness in everything again, running towards me. I thought the dancers were spinning around me. The frosted chandeliers on the ceiling came closer and moved away. As I rushed out, the waiters stopped and looked at me.

The big city surrounded me. If I stayed any longer in

its belly, to which I had long since become unaccustomed, I would suffocate. I jumped on the first bus that arrived and went in a random direction. As it was raining lightly, there was no one on the top floor of the bus. I went up and sat on the damp rubberised seats and seemed to recover a little.

People were still walking on the pavement below. The buildings on either side were hidden behind electric advertisements. Lights popping out of the windows of the dark houses clung to the trees along the street.

I reached out to the branches of these trees, which swayed above my head, stringing together. The leaves wet my fingers. A coolness spread over my whole body. Then I felt myself burning like fire.

The bus drove along increasingly lonely roads, increasing its speed in proportion to the desolation of the road. I had no particular destination, I just wanted to get away, away from this city that had suddenly intoxicated me and wanted to take me in its claws like a great living creature. As I moved away from the centre of Berlin and entered the outskirts, the asphalt streets ended and the pavement began. The bus moved forward with a slight jerk.

We stopped at a corner, the ticket seller came and told us we couldn't go any further. I got out and looked around, I didn't recognise any of the places. I just knew we were going to the south of the city, that was all. On either side were tall buildings with straight facades. While the bus was backing up, I walked around and suddenly heard music in the distance.

It was not the sound of a piano or house music that resounded from time to time from some window in Berlin onto the street. There had to be a place with music here. I searched it with my eyes, not to go in, but to pass it by.

Then, across the road and some distance away, I saw a place with lights shining on the road.

It was a cellar. After descending four steps, there was a low door. With the curiosity I felt at that moment, I descended the stairs, pushed open the door and went in.

The smell of liquor and damp air hit me in the face. Men with red faces sat at tables scattered around the edges of a recessed hall, occasionally raising large glasses of beer. In one corner, high in the air, a four-piece band (a piano, a cello, a violin and a drum) played the eternal tunes that never change in such musical places. I went to an empty table near the door and sat down. When I entered, I didn't see a coat rack, so I put my hat and some newspapers on a chair. I was brought a glass of beer. I began to look around. People, mostly workers, were sitting at tables with blue checked cloths, talking fast.

Occasionally the music would play a sixty-year-old waltz and burly men would pick up one of the drunken women at their table and start jumping up and down. The women, who wore an expression of boredom and depravity on their faces, smiled at the revellers who stepped on their toes. After the dance, the dark-haired man who played the cello performed his art on the piano. Then, one after the other, the not-so-inexperienced hands presented the pieces that made up the highest level of music here.

This "Barcarole", this "Nocturne", this "Hungarian Rhapsody" and "Carmen".... and the solemn expression on the faces of those who played them would have driven me away. But at that moment, a strange man entered.

First the door opened slightly and two light blue eyes wandered through the hall. Then, with timid steps, a small, thin body crept in. His anxious eyes roamed as if his gaze would offend those present, and he did not dare to sit down. I took my hat and newspapers from the chair beside me. When he saw this, he thanked me and sat down next to me.

Up close, it looked quite old. The corners of her eyes were wrinkled. His slender neck had wrinkles that reached the nape of his neck and his earlobes were hairy. When his eyes fell on me, he grinned as if to thank me, and his yellow teeth were visible between his thin lips. His eyes lit up briefly as they looked inside. I looked in that direction, a tall woman was coming towards us.

When she approached us, she greeted him in German: "Welcome, Gravila!" Then they spoke in a language I didn't understand. The woman pulled up a chair, sat down and continued talking. I noticed that they were not talking about a specific topic because they seemed to interrupt the conversation every now and then.

There was a strange melancholy in the woman's posture that made her already beautiful face even more attractive. But this, resembled the exterior of old and decaying castles and there was something of an eerie glamour about it. Her laugh did not make you laugh with her, but perhaps avert your gaze or even look away. It was as if something was hiding behind that smile.

All these things together tied one to her fate. I was already waiting for the moment of your departure with a barely restrained curiosity. I would immediately start asking the person next to me. But he stretched out his thin neck and clung to the woman in front of him with his eyes, as if he didn't want to leave her for an eternity if possible. He shook himself sometimes as if he were absorbing every word she said, and these words entered his body like a violent liquid.

After a while, the woman straightened up. After slapping the hand on the shoulder of the man next to me, she walked away with heavy but harmonious steps. At that moment, the sweet and pleading look in the man's eyes was replaced by a flaming passion. I shivered. I had never seen a man look at a woman so willingly, so madly, so desperately. I didn't dare ask him anything.

The woman sat down with some older and stouter men. Their appearance indicated that they were mediocre craftsmen away from home for a night. Every now and then, forgetting the woman next to them, they would get into an argument and the woman would fall asleep. The man next to me still had his eyes on her. Slowly, I offered him something to drink.

His gaze, which always wanted to say thank you, looked at me:

"I drink wine..." he said.

I called the waiter and asked him to bring wine for the man next to me. He looked at him with familiar eyes, and if I wasn't mistaken, he seemed to be smiling. It was not a very pleasant smile for me.

The man next to me poured himself a glass, drank it in one go, then said with a witty look:

"They know me here," he said, adding, "He's laughing because I found someone to buy wine for me again!"

I looked at him in amazement.

"There isn't always someone like her...", he said.

"I sit there all night without anything to drink and the landlord gets angry..."

Then he took another sip of the wine that clouded his eyes:

"Marina could also buy me something to drink, but she doesn't want me to get drunk. Because then she would have problems getting me home. His gaze wandered to her again and ignited as before.

I thought it was time to ask:

"Is she your girlfriend?"

"Yes!" he said.

But there seemed to be something hidden in this yes that I could not understand. I looked at his face. I looked at him.

"We are Romanians," he says. "And we have been together for six years..."

At this point, I felt a kind of rejection that comes when one is confronted with an ordinary case. However, when I thought about their behaviour towards each other, I realised that there must be further, incomprehensible and sinister aspects hidden behind this banality, which aroused my curiosity even more.

The man next to me had already started the second bottle. The fog enveloped the hall more and more. The tables emptied and the women's faces showed an increasingly obvious exhaustion. They had to shake themselves awake in order not to fall asleep at the tables.

The man at the counter sat on one side, his chin resting on his hand, lost in thought. The violin was playing "Toselli Serenade" for the hundredth time and the pianist was throwing his head back, trying to find the enthusiasm from the first time he played this piece.

The man, who had already half emptied the second bottle, put his hand on my shoulder:

"You are a strange person!" he said. "You don't speak, you don't ask questions. But you have such a way that you seem to understand everything."

He grabbed his collar with his hand and pushed the wine bottle. He wanted to say something.

He grabbed my hand on the table:

"I can't take it anymore..." he said.

"I can't stand it anymore ...", he said. "I can't stand it anymore. Tell me ... What do you want me to do?"

I withdrew my hand. He seemed to collect himself and looked ahead.

Then he said in a low voice:

"Forgive her... Forgive her. Oh my God, how I bother you..." he pleaded.

I calmed him down:

"Tell them to me," I said, "I will listen to them with interest!"

"Ah!... Not with interest... Listen to me with understanding... Have mercy on me. Achhh!..." he moaned.

Then suddenly, without any introduction, he began to narrate:

"Eight years ago... I studied at the University of Bucharest, I wanted to be a dentist. My father was a doctor in Constance. His situation was not bad. He could offer me a happy student life. I don't know if you have ever been there, but Bucharest is the happiest city in the world, the University of Bucharest is the happiest school in the world.... And I was the happiest student there.... Maybe also the cheekiest student. I also had a special influence on the women. I knew how to make them feel that I was not indifferent to them. I jumped from one to the other as naturally as a train leaving many stations behind.

But when I was in my last year, a little girl from Bessarabia managed to get me attached to her. We even moved into the same boarding house; she was a very flirtatious creature.

She didn't know what suffering was in the world. After we had lived together for a few months, winter came. I went to Constance. We parted without a trace of sorrow. I would return in fifteen days.

I arrived in Constance at noon. No sooner had I got off the train than I encountered a densely packed parade. I stopped and watched it. A lorry decorated with flowers drove between many people and in it stood a young girl in white clothes, almost still a child, greeting the people. On her head she wore a crown of honeysuckle.

I asked the people next to me.

"The beauty queen of Constance!" they said; As the first election of the queen took place this year, people were very excited and all of Constance was on its feet since last night.

I looked at the girl in the vehicle, her face was a little tired, a little surprised and a little happy. After the parade was over, I went home. That evening there was a ball in honour of the Queen. My friends wanted me to come in any case. I told them I was tired and so on, but they insisted.

You know, a decision made in a minute or even a second, a moment of hesitation, can have infinite consequences on a person's life. If I hadn't gone to the ball that day, if I had rejected with some force the not too strong urging of my friends, who knows what direction my life would have taken.

I went to the ball that evening and there was a great crowd. The queen was seen in the arms of another young man at every dance. She passed me several times. Her face was a little tired, a little confused and a little happy, as it had been the day before.

Later, I went to the buffet. Someone pulled me from behind. I turned around: one of my friends. Next to him was the queen.

She introduced us and then said:

"Wouldn't they give a student from Bucharest a dance?"

I started to turn and that was the first time I looked at this woman with attention. My feet seemed to wander and something inside me, a distant inkling, seemed to break. Her eyes were on me too. I didn't have the strength to say anything and struggled to regain my composure until the dance was over. We parted without a word. But during the following dances I learned that her name was Marina. She had been elected beauty queen while working in a grocery shop and those two days of fatigue had made her think about herself because she would start working again tomorrow.

She looked as if she wanted to wake up from this sweet but incessant dream. This state drew me closer to her. Probably because I had never seen such natural creatures around me, this girl seemed like a warm and quiet corner. Over the course of the next few days, I made a promise to see her again.

Why drag out these words, my Lord!... In short, I saw her every day after that night. The fifteen days I spent in Constance passed like an hour.

Oh, how I keep the memory of those fifteen days in my heart.... In those days I thought I could move the whole world with one finger. In those days, everything was possible for me.

If the whole universe and millions of years of life had no meaning, I thought these fifteen days could give them meaning. We walked side by side on the beach and just looked at each other and smiled. We walked in our coats where the waves licked the beaches and the wind circulated, kissing each other's cheeks reddened by the cold. But the fifteen days passed very quickly.

It was time to return to Bucharest. I had promised to marry her, but there was no way I could tell my parents. It would have been a risk to mention a girl who was first a shop assistant and then a beauty queen, a title sufficient to excommunicate her in bourgeois circles. I told her that I would pick her up as soon as I finished school, that I would then be independent and there would be no need to ask anyone. It wasn't right for her to come to the station, so we said goodbye the day before.

That moment is still in my mind. After we had hugged each other and cried for maybe half an hour, she called after me as we were leaving.

In a serious voice that I had not heard from her before:

"Don't separate from me... I'll be in a terrible way, Gravila!" she said.

I had never thought of the horror of this warning. But what did I know... How could I have known that it would come true so violently?"

Gravila paused for a moment. He turned his gaze to the woman dozing in the far corner, then reached for the wine glass and drank it down. Drops of wine dripped from his shaved chin onto his dirty shirt.

After pretending to wipe them with his hand, he continued:

"After I returned to Bucharest, we exchanged letters for several months, and each letter from her was more passionate. But I, in the happiest city in the world and among the happiest people in the world, could not remember the beauty queen of Constance as much as I should have. From my last letters I thought she must have felt this, and became sad. But she never wrote anything to suggest this. My letters became more and more irregular. Classes and friends kept me very busy, and the little Bessarabia girl with whom we had moved back into the same boarding house was obnoxious.

I thought she had started to forget me too, because after I had left three letters in a row unanswered, she too had stopped writing. I buried this adventure among other memories, but I was almost afraid to think about it, although the memory of it seemed like a beautiful thing.

University was over. I came here to Germany without ever having visited Constance to please my father and mother, who had arrived in Bucharest at that time. I wanted to get ahead in my profession.

The happy and pleasant days began again and lasted for a year and a half. Then I returned to Romania and went to Constance to get the money I needed to open a cabinet. In the meantime, a friend to whom I had anxiously inquired about the beauty queen told me that she had suddenly disappeared a long time ago. Oh, I said, fate wanted us to go our separate ways, what can we do? But how wrong I was. Oh, sir, if you only knew how wrong I was.

But I'm boring you, aren't I? Forgive me, I'm coming to the end.... Yes, when I returned to Bucharest with my father's money, some of us went to a music hall.

There I saw her, at the table of some drunken students. Her chest was open and she was drunk as a skunk. She didn't recognise me from a distance. When I approached her, she straightened up laughing. Then suddenly her eyebrows drew together. Her eyes blurred as if her drunken mind was haunted by many memories, and she bumped me on the chest with her hand and staggered away; she was never seen in the hall again that evening.

I was devastated. Since I couldn't stand it for long, I went back to bed and ran into the same music hall early the next night. She was there, as if she knew I was coming, and walked up to me without being surprised. They sat down at my table. We talked about this and that. But not a word did she mention her own situation or the old times. When I wanted to open the subject, she silenced me with a stern face and said:

"I have forgotten all the past days. I don't remember anything!"

I started going there every evening, and every evening these meaningless conversations between us repeated themselves. She talked to me like a friend, drank with me, danced with me, but she wouldn't let me touch the old thing, not a single word.

I felt myself falling madly in love with her again. I was fidgeting, like a man standing on the edge of a cliff about to fall.

With a last hope I asked her to leave this place and come to me; she only laughed, she laughed bitterly.

From then on, life became unbearable for me. Marina no longer stayed in one place, she travelled to different cities and countries. I dropped everything and started travelling with her.

She had no problems with that. She even took an interest in me. And she helped me. But nothing else... It was as if she wasn't a being of flesh, bone and sinew.

It was as if she were a marble, a stone or a dead person. Neither my screams nor my self-destructive attempts to repair the past helped. For six years now, this life, this hellish life has been going on. In these six years I have not once seen her heart soften towards me. As you have just seen, she is very interested and kind to me. But that is all. Once she has closed her heart, she never opens it again.

We stay in the same places, sometimes even in the same room. She knows how to build an invisible, cold wall between us.

I want her to be angry with me, to insult me, to hit me. I am ready to do anything, even kill myself. Only this overwhelming distance that stands between us, it should decrease a little. There were times when I thought I couldn't stand her any more, that I couldn't stand this life.

Then I wanted to put an end to it, but hope tied my hands. Sometimes I disappeared for days, I wanted her to think I had left her so that she would find another man.

On those days I always watched her from a distance. If I saw a man with her, if I saw her enter the house with another man, or if I saw her go to another man, I would be saved immediately, I would kill her and myself and put an end to this unbearable torment. But not once, Lord, not once have I seen her with another man. That really destroyed me... To know that she loved me, that she still loves me, that she loves me madly, that she can never love anyone but me.... But the thought that you can't forget what happened once, that living only for that is the most unbearable torture in the world for both of us.... Oh... if you only knew how much she loves me. I realise that. Don't you? Can't you see how she's torturing herself? What shall I do, Lord, what shall I do?"

Tears streamed from his light blue eyes.

There didn't seem to be anyone else inside. Marina slowly came closer. After examining me with her silent eyes, she grabbed him by the shoulders and shook him:

"Get up, Gravila, you're drunk again. How are we supposed to get home now?"

As if pinned down, she looked at the man, whose head was shaking from crying and shone through with an incomprehensible light, a radiance that resembled a secret affection. For a moment, a hint of sweetness appeared on her face, as if she were embracing him. But it had quickly disappeared. Now there was nothing on that face but the shattering melancholy I had seen before.

Oh God, this woman suffered so much.

I felt I had no strength left to watch this scene any longer and jumped up from my seat.

With a fleeting farewell, I threw myself out. The morning was approaching. I began to walk in a mist that gave my head a chill.

The great city, in all its complexity and infinity, slept quietly, hiding in its womb millions of people and adventures that did not resemble each other. Even for an imagination that went beyond the dark stone walls, this thought was terrifying. But was not the human heart even more complex and infinite than this city?

- Madonna in a fur coat -
Echo of Love Through the Ages
by Ince

Translation into German, corresponding to the spelling of Sabahattin Ali's poetry and prose in the original.

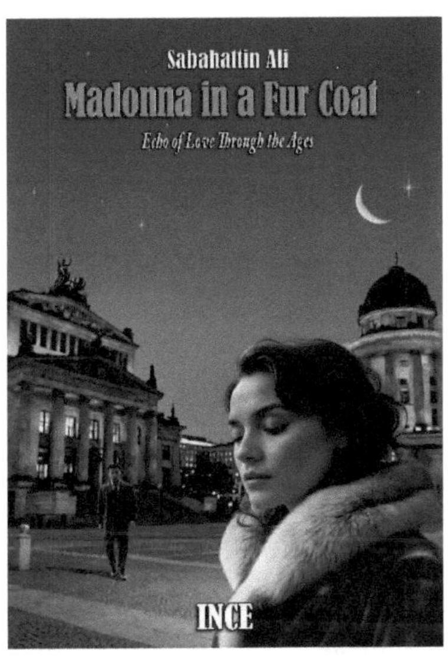

In the 1920s Berlin, Raif, an introverted, sensitive young man, meets an artist named Maria, whose intellect, independence and unwavering determination set her apart from her contemporaries. An intimate dance between love and self-discovery begins in a time full of change.

"Madonna in a Fur Coat" is a masterpiece of classical literature that has captivated readers all over the world for decades.

Demon Inside Us

Sabahattin Ali creates a vivid panorama of life in Turkey in the 1930s, exploring themes such as love, betrayal and the search for one's own identity.

This novel is not only a poignant love story, but also an astute commentary on the political and social challenges of its time, which is still relevant today. With its impressive narrative artistry, "Demon Inside Us" is a jewel of Turkish literature that is thought-provoking and touches the hearts of readers.

"The concise language and vivid characters make the book an unforgettable reading experience."